YOUR NAME IS WHAT?

by Joey Webster

illustrated by Luisa Padro

YOUR NAME IS WHAT?

by Joey Webster

illustrated by
Luisa Padro

YOUR NAME IS WHAT ?

A CHILDREN'S BOOK

WRITTEN BY JOEY "OCEAN" WEBSTER
CO-WRITTEN BY LANI, LOLO, & ALAYA
ILLUSTRATED BY LUISA "LULU" PADRO

COOL KIDS PUBLISHING

SYNOPSIS:

"Your Name Is What? " is a loving, fun-filled book full of laughs and life lessons.
In the book Joey's friend from GHANA comes to visit him in the United States.
Joey plans an amazing weekend for the two of them, except there's one problem... Everywhere they go, everyone seems to have a hard time saying his friend's name which leads to all kinds of trouble and laughs.

This is Joey's friends first time in the USA alone since summer, so young Joey goes to great lengths to make sure that his friend feels welcome in America. This is a funny story about the differences between them and the power that a name conveys.
Parents and Kids alike, will be entertained as they follow Joey and Matundee along on this adventure and discover just how interesting life can be when you have a unique name.

FOREWORD

GOD, you are exactly who you say you are. Thank you for your grace and mercy. It is my prayer that this book is a blessing to thousands of families and children around the world. AMEN.
This book was inspired by four of the greatest gifts that a man could ever receive. My wife Shelly, my daughters Ailani, Alora, and Alaya. To my right hand and partner in life, my wife Shelly, thank you for always supporting my dreams.

God knew exactly what to do when he sent me a wife that would not only follow me off a cliff, but one that would also help me crawl to the top. I love you and appreciate you more than words could express. To the authors of my life, comedians, love bugs, and my legacy - Ailani, Alora, and Alaya- you three keep Shelly and me laughing and truly make every day an adventure.

FOREWORD CONT..

A special thank you to my parents for always taking the time to read to us. I can still hear the dramatic voices and sounds that you would use to bring those characters to life. Your unconditional love and support throughout my entire life has been incredible. I thank God for you both.

To my little brother Patrick, thank you for being the first to show me what young fatherhood looks like and for making it look so cool. Thank you to my sister Gail. Thank you both for always being hilarious. Thank you for your tremendous strength and courage. To big brother Thadd, thank you for your support and loyalty. You've always been a true ride or die!

FOREWORD CONT..

To MOMA DOC, thank you for inspiring me to always be a student of life and thank you for encouraging me.

To my childhood friends, Mutaqee and Tareeq, it was a pleasure and an honor to have been a part of some of the expeditions behind the story and motivation for this book. Thank you for the brotherhood.

Hi I'm Joey.

"Now arriving. Flight D-97 from Accra on Ghana Air, Baggage Claim 4,"said the woman over the intercom. That's great news for me because that means that my bud from Ghana just landed.

This summer my best friend from Ghana is coming to stay with us for a few weeks. I'm excited. Ghana is in Africa. We've been best pals since kindergarten, I'm in third grade now so that means we've been friends for like...almost forever.

I've got all kinds of fun stuff planned. We are going to go swimming, play basketball, ride roller coasters .... you name it!

My mom and I drove to the airport to pick him up, but when we got there, we couldn't find him. I looked....Then looked some more. Just as I was getting tired and losing hope, I found the Ghana Air sign. Good gosh this is a high counter.

"Excuse me ma'am," I said.
Hmm. Maybe she can't see me. I know. I'll grab this suitcase "Excuse me ma'am."

Is this lady taking a selfie!!! Uhm...Hmmm EXXXXX CUSSSEEEE ME!! I'm looking for my best bud. His plane should have landed by now," I said.

"No problem. What's your bud's name?" she said. "Matundee (MAH -TOON- DEE)," I said. Okay, let me check... wait a minute...

"Uh... Your friend's name is

the woman from the airline asked.

I stood on top of a few suitcases and yelled, "MATUNDEEEEE," I said. But before I could yell it out again...

"Here I am," Matundee said, "Don't worry Joey, it happens all the time. I am used to it now."

Now that my bud is here, we can go to my favorite burger place. My mom says we only go there on special occasions. I'd say this counts and Mom agrees!

"Welcome to **SUPER BURGER,** home of the juiciest burgers in town," the man said. There are soooo many different burgers on the menu, but I already know exactly what I want. The man leans over and says "Go ahead with your order son."

"Say no more!", I said.
"I'll have the **jumping jack burger** with extra cheese and no mayo please," I said . Just saying the names alone is fun.

"Oh oh!!!" Matundee exclaimed with excitement, "I'll have the **junior can't stop won't stop** burger with extra pickles please."

The **SUPER BURGER** cashier turned to us and said, "Okay. No problem... I just need a name to call when your order is ready."

"Don't worry Joey. I gave him my name to call." Oh Snap!! I tried not to give him a blank stare and I really did my best to smile, but I already have a feeling that they're going to mess up our order.

10 minutes go by... 15 minutes...
Then 20 minutes. Ahh Man! This is what I was worried about. Excuse me sir, "Did you call the order for Matundee yet?"

"SAY WHAT?"

"What name???" the clerk said.

"MAH-TUN - DEE! Did you call it yet?"

"Oh... Ha...so that's what that was?" the cashier said.

"I thought someone made a mistake, we hadn't made your order yet," the burger guy said. The manager overheard our conversation.

"I'm sorry about the mistake kids," he said, "what if I make it up by giving you both free ice cream sodas while you wait?"

Awesome!!! We high-fived and forgot all about our cheese burgers.

The next day my mom took us to the soccer field to play with some of the neighborhood kids. One by one, I introduced my bud to all of the kids in the neighborhood.

I was very careful to make sure that I said his name slowly so everyone was able to say it. We were having so much fun. One of the kids on our team yelled, "Milwaukee kick the ball this way."

I quickly said, "hey!! that's not his name." Matundee kept playing, completely unbothered.

The next day my mom took us to the soccer field to play with some of the neighborhood kids.

One by one, I introduced my bud to all of the kids in the neighborhood.

I was very careful to make sure that I said his name slowly so everyone was able to say it.

We were having so much fun. One of the kids on our team yelled, "Milwaukee kick the ball this way."

I quickly said, "hey!! that's not his name." Matundee kept playing, completely unbothered.

The coach even yelled, "pass it to 'New-hockey'." Matundee scored the winning goal.

After the game the coach said, "yeah yeah man!! great moves New-hockey." My pal laughed and said, "My name is not New-hockey."

The coach turned brownish red with embarrassment, "OH I'm so sorry," he said, "How do you pronounce your name?" he asked.

"MAH-TUN DEE," he said.

The kids looked around. One of them said,

"YOUR NAME IS WHAT?"

Tommy the goalie said "Matundee."

The team cheered on -"Joey!! Matundee!!! Joey!!! Matundee !!!" We all laughed and celebrated our victory. On the way home, my little brother 'Pat Pat' was in the car and asked my bud, "Do you ever get tired of people messing up your name?"

He just laughed at us and said 'no'. "Why not?" my brother asked. "Well guys, my mommy and daddy chose that name for me, so its special and that means I'm special."

"Do you know what my name means?", Matundee asked. "No," I said.

"My name means 'One who is fruitful'." "Wowwww," I said. "Joey, your name is extra special as well," my mom said from the front seat.

REALLY? SAY WHAT??

"What does my name mean Mom? Cool kid of the World?" "I feel like that's probably close right?"

Mom laughed at me.
"Mom, what does my name mean?" I asked again.

"Your name means 'God will add to'."
Whoaaaaaa

Matundee and I looked at each other and screamed it again, "Whoaaaaa." "That's so cool," I said.

"Well, everyone's name may not have a meaning like yours, but it doesn't matter what people call you or if they can't pronounce your name correctly.

Everyone is special," my mom said. 'That's right," Matundee said.

"Whoaaaaa."
'That's so cool," I said.

Now, every time I meet someone, I'm going to wonder what their name means.

From then on, we never worried about correcting someone because they couldn't say our best friends' name.

He also never got upset if someone called him a bad name, because he knew that he was special.

COOL KIDS

Publishing Group, LLC

Printed in Great Britain
by Amazon

13730971R00020